I0572325

Dominik Shields asserts the moral right to be identified as the author of this work.

Paperback edition 2023
Cover design: Bethany McKay © 2023
ISBN: 978-0-646-87415-9

EBook edition 2023
ISBN: 978-0-646-87416-6

Published by Creative Inktuition -
brainchild of Dominik Shields.

This is a work of fiction. Names, characters, events and incidents are the products of the author's imagination. Any resemblance to actual persons, living or dead, or actual events is purely
coincidental.
Unless you want them to be real, then that's up to you.

***

I wish to acknowledge the Wurundjeri of the Kulin Nation on which this book was printed and written. I pay my respects to Indigenous Elders past, present and emerging.
It always was and always will be, Aboriginal land.

comfort & chaos

Dominik Shields

Other works by the author include -

Wither & Bloom (2021)
Sink or Swim (2022)

dedicated to all of us living in between a feeling.

comfort

You worship at my hips
your lips speaking the words of Evangelists
hands bound to a holy temple, from the mouth of you, babe, I
come undone.
Psalm to palm, movement is gentle, fingertips experimental
a passion, a pride, you hold out on the borderline just for one night
I acquiesce only the best parts of my heart,
grip tight, I'll be the Saviour to show you the light.

A HEART IN HALVES

You hold your heart in halves
you hold yourself in two parts
a trickling soul ending up in the middle.
I hold my heart in halves,
Yours lies within my chest
I keep it there, a place to rest,
a place to call home.

I keep my heart in halves, so that yours doesn't know how it feels to
split in two,
because against my better judgement
I fell in love with you.
My heart is held in halves,
with love for myself, with love for another,
my heart is in halves,
holding what I know to be true -
my love for myself runs as deep as my love for you.

Darkness holds us tender in her arms
my eyes watching a film, sadness on a big screen,
yours absorbing me and the way my glasses fog,
the sides of your mouth curling into a smile,
strong fingers hold mine tighter, at least for a little while.

I thought I was the only one to steal glances at you,
then I realised you were sneaking them too.

KINDRED SOUL

I feel as if I have known you
once or twice before, we have met already in another vessel.
I did not need to explain
the convoluted thoughts that resided in my brain
because you knew them just the same.

I'm a tourist in my own life, you're the city that I left behind.
Disorientation will enrich your life's vacation,
for you will return home without first seeking salvation.

I curl myself in bed and watch the lightning as it rages overhead,
my thoughts wander to if you can see it, if it still has the same affect on you.
Do you hear the thunder? The growl of its throat grows louder,
I wish my voice would wake the heavens and crackle upon the earth
maybe then they would finally hear me.
Crack me open, my throat will expose the curse that follows me by day,
only by flashes of lightning will it be spread, ears unable to block out what I
have been trying to say.

LOVE YOU TO DEATH

This relationship is one that cannot be described
by you or I, my friend
it had no real beginning and I know that it has no end,
until the Reaper comes to claim us both
our sorrows then turn to joy,
for we will be able to rest without worry
knowing that our souls spilled into one another
without having to wonder
how we got here.

Her jeans were blue and her top was red
I've been dreaming about her for weeks on end
who is this woman with hair chestnut brown,
that I cannot get out of my head?
The way she would glide
how her hands fell by her sides
a coy look upon her face,
chipped black paint upon her fingertips.
I see her when I close my eyes,
I see her smile - a constant in my mind.

Bundle me up when it's freezing cold, tell me what it's going to be like
when we get old.
How we'll laugh, how we'll love - when our hearing is gone and we
can't see much.
Tell me how you'll ease the pain, when all that's left of me is skin and
dark blue veins.

I wear your locket around my neck
time ceases to forget
our life together was heaven sent.
A gentle, silver reminder of you
glimmering purple and azure blue,
you once held my heart
I held yours too.

I always seem to write about how wonderful love is although my heart
is breaking
I suppose this is the only thing that keeps my knees from shaking -
I write these with truth and for all of you
so that you can learn from the mistakes of this little romantic fool.

I fall asleep with you in my ears
a headphone crackle
lingering pauses.

Quiet breath, a midnight laugh.
It's not long distance. It's just bad timing.

Stitch my heart upon your sleeve, I'll stitch yours upon mine
maybe we'll be able to make it work this time.

My darling moonbeam
my little daydream,
I have been waiting to kiss you,
longing to hold you,
do you feel the same way too
or am I wasting my love on you?

What you're seeking will come in time
when you erase me from your mind, you will find the parts that you've
had to hide.
Sunshine will kiss the deepest parts of your darkness, you will feel
content in your growth, your ever changing journey that only you can
take.

Be still upon the ground you tread, you never know what may laying
ahead - joy and sorrow, an opportunity you can follow, a new person,
a vision, something reserved just for you upon your mission.

I'm learning to embrace the world as my dog does
through smell, gentle touch and basking in the glow of morning sun.
Eternally optimistic that your world is good as the people within it,
walking is slower, running toward what I want with enthusiasm
grass is greener with a friendly demeanour
I kiss my friends and lovers as equals.
Through her eyes I do not see comparison -
I see joy, wonder and an everlasting possibility each morning.

I swim in the rivers of the world even if they are cold,
bursting with excitement when I wake,
a full heart and belly when I sleep,
no longer will I let anxiety be the thief of a life worth living.

CHAPEL OF LOVE

Lonesome wedding dress
did you spill champagne on your wedding guest?
I wonder if it ever met Elvis,
a glitter-clad suit
asking if they'll love each other the most,
when the folks are gone and there's nothing to toast.
Fools rush in,
a hunk of burning love now just a hunk of someones burning junk.
Discarded.
Unlike the love that filled the seams at the wedding of one persons
dream.

This morning I spent thinking of you -
the fraying of your shorts
and the hole in your shoe.
My coffee went cold, my toast did too
forgetting love was never taught,
it's just something we naturally do,
for I spent most of this winter morning
thinking of you.

You deserve better than to be put secondary by someone who is
sedentary in their love for you -

You are not the secretary, scheduling plans or appointments with the
one anointed to your heart, your existence should not be met with
resistance by another.
You should not be governed by one with a persistent
ever-changing mind, by someone who cannot find the time to love
you as you deserve, that is your right.

You are the sunshine, our ray of light. You are someone made up of
strength and might, you are delicate, but not to be fucked with.

You are soft and you are strong. It was them that has been living wrong.
You are the summertime and the strength of your love is like
hurricane, you are not a burden nor are you a pain.
They should be eternally grateful that they ever had the chance to
speak your name.

I wish that we never met because then my brain wouldn't have to forget and I wouldn't keep getting the same questions from your friends.

If we'd never met, I wouldn't have black scuffs on my shoes, I wouldn't have to cry in my room and there would be less fragility where my heart used to be.

Our lips wouldn't crack in the exact same place, I wouldn't have to forget your face, perfect teeth, your birthmark and the other half of a missing piece.

Imagine if we'd never met, we'd be bored to death.

Long to hold the hand of a lover who doesn't keep you undercover,
dip into the pool of love and admiration made for you, bask in the
light of someone who keeps you up at night - for reasons right.
Long for the lover who comes home, without sins to atone, one who
won't make you feel all alone.

SAD BOY: ONLINE

You made a joke about a celebrity dying I thought you were serious
and almost started crying,
you said I made you happy, filled you with joy, it filled you to the brim.
I could imagine your smile setting off your eyes which compliment
your chiselled jaw and chin.

A late night conversation that started with cannoli, I couldn't have
predicted it even if you'd told me.

There's something in the way you speak, how you reluctantly told me
your big three, even though I know you don't believe in astrology, yet
you knew it would make me smile and keep the conversation going
on for a little while.

There's something about this that makes me come undone,
sometimes I am awake while you sleep,
you lost in stillness and peace,
there is a tranquility when you dream,
I'm scared to death, unable to hold my breath, my head a mess,
I've searched for something that will make sense of how this
happened so fast, both of us dragging the baggage of our recent
past.
We thought we could just leave our ghosts at the door, not have
them scamper across a wooden floor, trying to break through the
wall.

Kiss me again, no need to pretend,
this had no real start date and we don't want it to end,
keep me close and our hearts will begin to mend,
a love, a bestfriend,
our pasts we will transcend.

Sydney came and Sydney went
solitary days were heaven sent
I stayed out there on my own
but still made time to phone back home.
I watched a sunrise and then the sun set
I gave out as much as my heart would get,
kissed new faces of humans and pets,
took time away from chaos,
to learn where the authentic me begins.

SONGBIRD

There are a handful of songs that remind me of you
I'd sing them all, if you ask me to,
my voice would break, lungs would shake
it would be more than either of us could take.
I'd sing them till I went blue in the face
for my head and heart are finally in one place
melodies sum it up better than I could say -
how I've ended up loving you this way.

The scent of you lingers in my sheets
or the memory at least
of how you would put my mind and body at ease,
early mornings spent together, the secrets we keep
eyes blurry trying to keep them focused on me.

Take me somewhere I've never been
show me something only your eyes have seen
it won't matter if the tide is rough or the forests serene
or if the park not pristine.
I want to see what you've seen,
learn who you are, where your feet have tread,
the places that help clear your head.
Spread your arms, your old self you can shed,
show me something new, I'll bring something blue
to our place, somewhere we can bloom.

I love you
in every way
the shape of you, how your hair would curl, how you sleepily say my
name,
you - the oxytocin in my brain.

We hid in the gully
away from the voices that echoed
we weren't in trouble or on the run
we were just young, foolish, in love.

APRIL, FOREVER

I remember the first time we met, you talked a mile a minute.
Your eyes were wide and your arms waving off beat while your
anxious feet kept perfect time. The weather was beginning to change,
we were on the ground of our best friends place.

I saw you a handful of moments after that. Each time more erratic
than the last. You were evading something from your past.

One night you stood up so abruptly, your stool creaking in the silence
of a band playing in front of you. You were so loud, waving me over,
wanting me to sit down, take your seat, *you'll have a better view here,*
your smile so big how could I resist?

Your nails were blue, I couldn't take my eyes off of you, I braided your
hair and you, with a laugh so gentle, patiently sat there.

You drove me home, calmer now, I made you a cup of tea, you
were so serene, it was then you sang to me.
I jokingly called you a teenage dream, you blushed, I felt my heart
rush.

I'm not sure if it was the seltzer, the way the moon kissed us through
the window or if I felt deep down it was going to be you.

Your name leaves my throat in a whisper.
I'm afraid if I speak it too loudly, too often, you will disappear,
figure of my imagaination, a reverse apparition.

SOMETHING

There is something in the way -
you took the time to remember the foods I cannot consume,
I told you not to worry about it, you just looked at me and said *'I
don't want to accidentally kill you.'*

A bamboo toothbrush sits in your bathroom drawer *'just in case,'*
how your eyes light up when you find something amusing or a new
adventure to chase,
you speak to me like springtime rain, yet your laughter can echo
through a crowded room, bringing joy all the same.

I see how you love your friends so deeply, their pain and joy are yours,
you hold them so delicately, saying goodnight with an *'I love you, text
me when you get home.'*
There is something in the way that you romanticise melodies and
the way music makes you feel, showing those closest to you affection
with *'this song reminds me of you.'*

Sleeping with a heater on in the corner of my room reminds me of
you.
How you can't sleep without sound, the quiet freaks you out.
You used to listen to my heart beat, the noises I made in my sleep or
the drumming of your fingers against my tucked knees.

Sun rises, the magpies call, dew melts and coffee hits the
bottom of locally made ceramic mugs.
Mornings are slow and I am greeted with a kiss, first one dog
and then another, whipping tails banging against the wardrobe
door, *'good morning, hello, time to play ball!'*

There are bees outside my window, they kiss blooming lavender
- to and fro their little wings continue to go, it must be so simple
to live this way.

I wish to live in a tiny body, moving so quickly from one thing
to another, with boundless energy, and freedom as the light of
the morning covers me.

Whizzing past pine and brambles, there isn't any time to amble,
sweet work has begun, haven't you heard?

Spring has sprung.

BREAKFAST IN MAY

You looked up places where I could get pancakes in your
neighbourhood because I couldn't stop thinking about them.
Legs brushing, cutlery clashing, breakfasts are meant for
sharing.
One coffee, then two, pancakes on our list of things to
eventually do.

You always know the right thing to say even if you think
otherwise,
you listen deeply with your heart and your hands
energy gentle, sentimental, the one who understands.

Yet, you're still confused as to how I got myself into this mess.

THE HILL

You said it was a peculiar feeling
laying on your kitchen floor, staring up at your own ceiling,
you hadn't looked at your house from this point of view but
were happy to share it with someone new.
We looked for the cracks, our fingers touching at the sides, your
laughter low as a cooling breeze came through an open window.
You turned onto your side, eyes hazy and smile wide, you told
me there was an opportunity you thought you may have missed,
I shrugged my shoulders with a smile, hands moving to yours by
an inch, feeling a mile,
you shuffled in your space, falling and losing your place, that
smile never leaving your face,
midnight in a drunken bliss,
both of us waiting to be kissed.

Aphrodite whispered to the wind, words fall on the ears of young lovers,
lightly touching the parts of them kept covered.
A sun shone bright, new love burning bright, even the haze of summer could not set hearts alight.
Midas could not have constructed anything gleaming and gold that would make their love fold - their insecurities upon new feelings left untold.
From you to me, love slipped into our bloodstream' they spoke these words so softly, giving in to a hearts desire never costly.
Winds blew, from days nights grew, Gods watched from a distance, faith in young love starting anew.

I love watching people hug in the street -
how long ago was it since you were last able to meet?
Tell me what I've missed, who was the last person you kissed?

Your place
my toothbrush
six months
'just in case.'

You say *love you* as easily as stating the time, as calmly as asking
about the weather.
It's easy to love the way you do,
I wonder if you'll ever mean it in the same way
when I smile and say *love you too.*

They say that good things take time
they come to those who wait
so I knew that I was right in holding out for you,
we always said we would end up fine.
You kept your promises and I kept to mine
maybe it was timing
maybe it was fate
I knew we would find each other
if our hearts were willing to wait.

OH, LOVER

Lover, you were not fodder
for my little rhymes
you captured my heart and both my eyes.
Oh, lover, I wish you could see
how you meant more to me
than midnight smiles and sun-kissed cheeks.
A rose-tinted vision to everyone else,
a long-term possibility to me,
just as the sun makes frost melt
we are what could have been, with the cards we were dealt.
Oh, my lover,
you have made it impossible to fall for another,
but I must carry on
for I do not have the energy to stay and suffer.

SOFT LANDING

You held my cheeks in your hands,
warm against my frozen skin, soft jazz hummed from the
speaker in your kitchen
your smile gentle and wide, a little black dog sat by my side,
a chance in the dark, inklings of a spark,
whiskey lips and midnight partnerships - the beginning of a
heart's eclipse.

One p.m on Tuesday as I sat looking out of the second story
watching as a single man drank wine
he did not have a suit or tie,
just a shirt as neon as the morning sky,
he wore a smile, a manicured moustache adorned his face
I wanted to sit beside him, soak in his space, find out what
made him first glide into this place.

One delicately held roses for his lover
while the other tearily said goodbye to his significant other
they both watched as trains departed
one towards the countryside
one towards a lover's destination already charted.

OLD FRIEND,
WE MEET AGAIN

I watched as they put a casket into a hearse,
the day was wet, the temperature worse,
humid and claggy, Priest's robes drowning in water, ripped and
tatty,
it was a funeral to which nobody came and reminded me that we
would all be ending up the same -
buried in a box or floating upon the breeze,
all the turmoil and trouble of our life now at ease.

SOUTH BY SOUTH WHATEVER

Austin called your name
the mystery of a new city, true happiness you could not feign,
kindness marked your new reign.
You flew over state lines, a heart wrapped up with twine
you passed by desert and sandstone, past the crowds and all of
the lights,
you wish you had time to spend alone.

Texas called and your soul began to roam, to understand what
you wanted you had to leave the safety of home.
There was something about a barren terrain that made you want
to stake a claim,
you came back changed, a new version of yourself you didn't
have to fake.

I'm proud of who you were and who you grew to become,
I don't think you would have been able to find your new home
without leaving your old life in ruin.

Softly at the cemetery, we joke about where we would like to be buried -
Not close to the road, it's too loud
I don't want to be under the oak, in case it falls on me.

I'd like a quiet space, one where I can hear my thoughts,
somewhere I can finally breathe,
somewhere that isn't encouraging my mind to race,
I'd like somewhere soft, somewhere warm,
somewhere that reminds me of autumn, without leafy maelstrom.

I'd like somewhere that feels safe, a gentle breeze, a prime piece of real estate
'You'll still be paying rent when you're dead.'

That may be the case, but at least I'd like to enjoy the landscape.

NOBODY HAS ME LIKE YOU DO

My mind is a mess,
my heart was too,
I closed myself off,
then you came out of the blue,
you encouraged me to try, to see where it could go,
the broken pieces fixed up with glue,
we are taking our time, keeping things slow,
a low key endeavour, a love that might be true,
I didn't think it could happen
especially this soon,
nobody has come close,
nobody has me like you.

Through time and open space, something landed in a thought
out place, through it's own means of travel
unblemished knees fell upon the gravel.
It held out its hands, open and waiting, seeking something there
for the taking.
There was no beginning and no end, round and round it wound,
connected and bound with golden thread.

There flaws and gaping holes but it was held so tight, in a small
ball, it kept itself shut with all of its might.
Nothing fell out, so delicately it would hold. For days it did not
move, nowhere to go nothing to prove.

The hands cradled it gently, for days and through nights, it
started to grow softer in the autumn light.
Day by day the thread fell away,
inside, untarnished,
the love of the world, waiting in earnest.

I have been waiting for you, it said with a smile,
the love from its hands, spreading from coast to isle.
Watch as it goes, slowly at first, watering your eyes and
quenching your thirst, it is not where you expect nor does it
come when you think, keep your heart open, it can be gone in a
blink.

Sat back to back
books in hand
snacks in their backpack
turning pages their soundtrack.

BACK TO YOU

The marks on my shoes, the fraying of my jeans, holes in my
jacket, it means nothing without all of you.
I found a home in beautiful faces, in places I thought I'd never go, I
left the safety of myself tucked away in case I needed to find it.

I opened myself up to the world, I walked the roads that I dared
tread, snow kissed my lashes and sun darkened my skin,
the old and new, I'm not sure where one ends and the other
begins. I let my heart speak the truth, I let my eyes cry for the ones
that needed proof, I left you all behind so that I would be able to
be washed anew.

I always come home to the ones that make me feel the safest:
the ones who let me into their nooks, into their private spaces. I
let parts of myself go, I had to do it on my own, reinvent what I
defined as a home, I came back to all of you.

LAND OF THE SUN

It always feels like coming home whenever I see you
there is a safety and comfort in the way you say
'have you had your coffee yet?'
A perfect morning,
two coffees,
my sunshine,
you.

From one lover to another
you know I never wanted to be a bother
I wanted to be a place where you can feel safe
my arms wide open just like a shelter
from lover to lover
I know that you haven't eyes for another.

I didn't know you as well as I thought I did,
what I thought was a curse,
turned out a blessing,
as I grew to learn,
I grew to love
a person,
effervescing.

I love you, I love you, I love you
tumbles through my chest
just as stallions stampede through the West.

Should we carve our names into the old oak tree
so they stay everlasting?
Unbroken by time, undisturbed by the havoc of human nature,
kept there forever
even after the leaves are gone,
after our memories fade,
our bones are cradled once again by the earth.

HOT & HEAVY

Taking my time with you
slow and steady -
we can't afford to be hot and heavy,
we're in no rush,
safety in my lovers touch,
bedsheets are just enough.

GREY

Will you still love me when I'm far away
when my eyes are dulled to the lightest of grey
when my hair no longer looks the same and when my throat is
unable to croak out your name?

HALLOWEEN

I creep you out
you creep on in
under my fingernails, under my eyes, my skin.
I don't know where I start and we begin
how is it that you get into all of my creases
find your way into my niches,
always on my mind, always in between.

You wear your mask and I wear mine,
it's Halloween,
our crushes hidden underneath,
you were always out there looking for me,
trick or treat.

KISSY GIRL

She did not ask for the world
wanting only for quality time just between the two of you,
space reserved for lips undisturbed,
a smile would curl at the sides of a mouth waiting to be kissed,
over and over she tried to keep you on her side,
with a tongue so tied,
she let out a wish,
the heavens obliged,
teeth finally clashing in the night.

Planes flew overhead, the noise came and went, the sky broke open as they left.
High above the ground, for them nothing but a dull humming sound. I wonder where they go, are they headed for fun or are they simply returning home? Do they leave something behind or are they seeking something they weren't able to find?

We are able to escape as quickly as the wind changes, we leave behind our lovers, friends and neighbours. What a joy it is to see the world, feel the presence of some place new, to discover different parts of you.
Where will you go? Who will you see?
I can't wait for you to live at your truest frequency, freed from the shackles of what they told you to be.
Live up in the air, I'll be here on the ground, awaiting your safe return and to hear of all the new things you have found.

Gin stained lips, hips littered with marks from your ink stained fingertips, melted wax and secret partnerships.
It is the night that breeds new life, it is the weight of you that makes me feel alright.

Go on, set me alight.

Kisses where your teeth collide,
embraced wholly by the one at your side.
An easy Tuesday morning, where an I love you comes without
warning when covers replace clothes and you are pressed nose to
nose.

LOVE LASSO

Wrap me up in your love lasso, hold me tight don't let me go. I've been fighting against my head and against my chest for something I should have trusted from the start, trust in a lover who makes you laugh, who keeps his word and follows his heart.

Although one hurt you once before doesn't mean you need to close the door on something your soul needs, that gives you a break from grief.

SCORPIO SUN, PISCES MOON

She's exactly as I thought she'd be
gentle, sweet
strawberry hair and rosy cheeks,
the best thing to ever happen to you
a new lifelong best friend
for your sweet wife, for you a light of my life,
she is my Scorpio sun, my Pisces moon,
and I have the privilege of watching her bloom.

She will grow,
plans and dreams she will sow,
her heart will love and it will hurt
she will be built strong, like her mama taught her to be,
eyes so wide, a mind so alert,
she will move quickly, of lovers she will be picky,
she will guide and she will lead,
a balanced, ascending Libra she is sure to be.

Kiss me under the shade of the trees,
as the sun goes down and the heat sinks into our bones,
your hands in my hair, tracing my collarbone, your hands
everywhere.

The hazy scent of summer, birds dancing across a tangerine sky,
excited dog barks harmonise with the song of crickets.

Red blossoms with green leaves fall at our feet, socks covered
in grass, lips lazy.
Push away thoughts of work tomorrow, pleasantly present
with you, silent together, sighs falling into the green thicket.

My head is a mess, I'm constantly restless, I feel like my brain has
tipped out from the center of my chest. There is a gnawing in my
stomach, so loud I can't ignore it, it calls me at night, it finds me
in the morning. I can feel my heart race, my dreams no longer
the ones being chased, life becoming fast paced.
A heart reeling from a past feeling, one tied up in a lover who's
heart was not true, one who did not feel the same for you.
Slowly I learn to trust in change,
watch how things unexplained become the maker of days,
how eyes are set ablaze,
my past self unphased.

HOW TO LOVE YOU

after our first kiss you asked about my love languages
touch and quality time
you told me you aligned with touch and words of affirmation
good thing I'm a writer then
you laughed and kissed me again
then your lips let slip
and my hands will always make the time for you.

APPLE PIE

I fell in love with a boy as sweet as apple pie
he always made me laugh, he never made me cry
his wit was quick and his humour dry,
my stomach would hurt,
exhausted days were always worth
sleepless nights.

We did not fight, he did not lie,
he made me feel as if I was precious as a gilded sky
he was as safe as he was shy,
he made my heart melt, my brain and creativity come alive,
when his hands touched my skin, I knew it was going to be him,
he had a velvet soul and love in his eyes,
he was as sweet as apple pie.

LOVE IS A WOMAN

It's you, my love, you,
how beautiful it is to feel the safety of us two.
Can you button up my jumpsuit?
Can I come over and cry to you?
Did you need to borrow my shoes?

I cried and you did too,
covered in blankets snuggled into your sofa,
our hands wrapped together, legs tangled between socks and
shoes,
remember, you were never his,
it's his choice lose someone as wonderful as you.

I love you in the morning and into the late afternoon,
you held me when I was high and when I fell low,
you saw me as I was then and who I have grown into.

COLD BREW & YOU

Morning light, a kitchen knife, sunbeams through the kitchen
window,
soft breeze moves dancing plants, candles covered in melted
wax,
it's the sound of construction, it's the scent of you,
a hand grazing my back and soft funk from the other room.

It's slow mornings with a lot to do, a cold shower then lacing up
dirty shoes,
down to the market, a walk to the park, hand in hand, lips kissing
my arm,
too good to be true, my brain is sounding the alarm.

Cold brew and you, kissing on the carpet in the late afternoon,
my head is dizzy, my stomach feels sick,
uh oh, I think you might be it.

He sang me Jeff Buckley

his voice rang out into the night so softly

you've been on my mind

his left hand grazing my thigh

the roads were quiet, the moon was high

you've been on my mind

we wound through the streets, his fingers drumming to the beat

our voices over each other, one thought to occupy

'so, do you want to stay at mine?'

We walked inside, our voices hushed and feet light,

I still remember the way to your room, down the hall and on
the right,

I thought I felt us growing colder, then you kissed my neck and
shoulder

oh, I'm glad I came on over.

In a beer garden
under a summer sky
they sat gazing upon the others eye,
their first I love you
softly spoken, not simply a token
over a pint or two
anxiety easing
as the daylight became the moon.

HI, DARLIN'

The way you said it was slow and charmin'
a gentleness that was disarmin'
you wore a cowboy hat with beat up sneakers,
the moonlight softened your features,
I felt my walls slowly come apart,
I didn't think it could be done,
by a sweet talkin' smoking gun.

The Northside cowboy,
he tried to play coy,
stumblin' over his words sometimes,
but whenever he picks up the phone
his voice calm and low, I know him to be true
whenever I hear him say,
'hi darlin', I can't wait to see you.'

ELENA

You taught me how to laugh again
how to find joy and play,
you showed me the world wasn't as bad as the one in my head
and people were a lot better than those I kept letting into my
bed.

It was flowers on a Monday afternoon
coffee in the park, a new friend or two
'Babe, you should do it, you have nothing to lose!'
Ethereal and kind,
a true knowing of my mind,
my compass and my third eye,
a true love in the purest of forms,
my sweet friend, from now till we begin life again.

My head lays upon your chest
my face between your cupped hands
the space where it fits best,
a summer breeze
'do you want to dance?'
I am bursting at the seams,
leaping at every chance,
to spend these moments with you, when we have made plans
or have nothing to do.
An open hearted space, a place for memories to be made,
a grin on your face, arms wrapped around my waist,
our road not yet laid, my lips pressed to your forehead,
maybe it was never them, it was you I was meant to find
instead.

TO BRUNSWICK, WITH LOVE

Sydney Road is where my heart found a home,
it was vivacious and kind
magic made under streetlamps at night,
secrets kept, hearts broke, we wept,
always paint that's wet.

The smell of coffee, an international roast,
the way a man would reminisce about his beautiful wife,
he tells me of their love, their children and their loving life.
My soul opened here, friendships bloomed in dusty rooms,
screaming at the top of our lungs, watching the full moon.

It gave me a boy with a sweet face and dreams to chase,
it gave my friends and I a place to roam,
margaritas at someone's show,
it held me close then it let me go
always with the space for me to come back home.

You sang me Sinatra, you sang me Elvis,
you made me think I was worthy of feeling like this,
open, beautiful, worth the risk.

Dancing by candle light,
beneath a star filled sky,
in your newest op shop find,
you spun around, your eyes clear and bright,
a breeze cold, I sat fireside,
you are so beautiful, a sight to behold.

LUNAR EMBRACE

She hangs low over you, breathing down your spine, a cool touch, early morning rush.

Holding you close. Holding your heart delicate.

Silver and blue, she only has eyes for you.

Stay soft, the darkness in your head she will fight off.

My heart has never been deprived of love
even when the feeling has been too much,
it holds onto goodness
it is an endless well,
pouring out from heaven to the pits of hell
in a vain hope that I will be able to convey,
the amount of warmth and tenderness
given to me every single day.

I knew myself best
when I let the layers fall away
as if I were getting undressed
from the version of myself that I used to be.

Both of us are sick of this town, baby, how does Colorado
sound?
A snow capped mountain, another opportunity presenting,
we can leave our cares behind, we can finally get offline.
We can see the Rockies, babe
I haven't felt at home since I left the plains,
the everlasting landscape,
the way the skies would change,
how the wind would whisper my name.

We can live by the lake, marvelling at you, your shape,
the way you shine in this place.
A cabin and you, firewood for two, black coffee in the shade
of the afternoon,
we can escape to Colorado,
pack up the van and the dogs,
the hills are calling our name, the Dakota's too,
just tell me when you're ready to go.

The world is quiet as we walk side by side
her on my left
then on my right,
we take life in our stride,
she is the comfort within the chaos of my mind.

Snow dripping off the eaves in Hamstead Heath
it smells like Christmas Eve,
frozen hands tucked into festive sleeves
snow crunching under feet.
Will you kiss me under the mistletoe
or will this year be under the tree?
Yellow lights line the boutique,
a gift for you, one for me,
don't forget to send a card to Emily.

At home, I made something warm and boozy
oh,
I ruined the surprise, I'm sorry.

Will you still walk the streets with me,
even when the sleet is soaking our shoes,
I didn't think I'd be having Christmas with you.

Hand in hand with you at this time of year,
one more house to visit,
promise,
then I'm all yours.

HEADFIRST INTO FEELINGS

Racing towards something that started out as a little bit of fun,
something that once made you turn your back and run,
you are now facing towards the one you love,
your saturn, your sun, the one who makes your mind come
undone.
Diving head first into the unknown,
the one you cannot stop thinking about,
a love that you're allowing to grow
even though it was scary at first
you let your sadness burst,
happiness takes reign.

It's mid November and you're still here
I thought that you would have been gone by now,
taken away with the wind and sound, the holiday cheer creeps
near.
You tell me you'll be home for Christmas,
you'll be under the tree, wrapped up like the rest of my
presents,
your heart was in it, your smile held
it wasn't until I landed on the ground,
that I realised how hard I fell.

Let it seep out of me
like the sap does the trees
like the rivers to the valleys
the songs of the canaries,
one song wrapped up within me,
all thanks to you.

NEVER DEAD IN NEVADA

A city where the dead don't keep, their souls aren't left to sleep,
it's bright lights, it's lightning strikes, there's friction on the
streets.
We swelter, tourists seek shelter.
Dust rolls through, come and gone in an afternoon, flamingos
in the Sands, its eternal night life.
Take a look through desert eyes, don't let the good times pass
you by,
Bogart, Sinatra, it's the sight of Freemont Street,
feeling lucky baby, wanna roll with me?

A little apartment filled with trinkets made up of you, every
corner showing your truth, vintage furniture and modern art.
Stacks of books, records in a pile,
you say you don't like to own a lot of things,
they just get in the way, you say it with a smile,
while unboxing another thing that means a lot to you.

Eating breakfast in the hum of the mid afternoon,
a city shrieks below, I thought living this way would be hollow,
there is a strange comfort in being so high above the ground,
in the safety of you,
incense burning throughout the room.

A skyline, a steady horizon,
cocktails stirred not shaken,
I've never been in this position
of knowing someone so well, yet not at all,
a mystery to unravel, kiss me quick,
before you leave again, your soul set to travel,
leave a piece of you at home with me, here in this buttercream
room.

SALT & CINNAMON

Left the comfort of the world that you were living in,
the friends you made, the love that you gave,
all for the thrill of a new chase. A new place, beginning a new phase,
your eyes and heart seeking a new face.
The stars aligned, as did your energy and mind, you found
people you weren't seeking to find, you now settled into your space.
Rain was calling, the cold was too,
wrap yourself tight, there is nothing here for you to prove,
everyone is so proud of you,
so, maybe, you have found the place you always meant to.

SLOW BURN

Life can feel *now now now*
an urgency for what's next
we forget to slow down,
we do not realise the power of no,
the strength in letting things go,
how much we can achieve when we let our mind wander,
when we take stock of what is in front of us, for just a little
longer.

Your life is meant to be cherished,
not rushed,
merely working then waiting to perish,
settle into where you are, then love what you see,
you are here, you are alive, you are meant to live wholly.

I have seen every sign on the roads from here to Bristol,
they always end up leading me back home,
back to open arms and gratitude filled hearts,
of lovers near and far apart,
chosen family and those connected by blood,
never questioning what you've done,
they hold you when times get rough.

SAINT VALENTINE

Foster the love between the both of us,
from skin and bone
to this little place that we have called our home,
harmony is what you condone
for two souls no longer wishing to be alone.
Saint Valentine,
carve out the time
for a love we do not have to fein,
one that will continue to reign
long after we have gone.

January brought with it the heat of a summer rain, it was calm,
it called me by name, then there was you,
bounding through the suburbs with no need to explain.
You showed up exactly as you are, open and undone,
carrying the feelings left behind by an old someone.

I drank in the sight of you,
fought off the idea that these feelings weren't true, they were a
fallacy, not worthy of someone with as much baggage as me.
You made me feel alive, you made me want to try,
I was finally starting to understand my mind,
it was the summer of you, the summer of us,
your hands in mine, no need to run,
it was the summer rain that made me come undone.

LONG DISTANCE LOVER

The shape wrapped up in your sheets,
a scent you follow behind as you walk in the streets,
it's the toothbrush on the side of your sink.
Traces littered around your spaces,
the cafes you idle in,
the park where you thought about giving them your ring.

You hold onto them delicately,
a thread weaving continent to continent,
feelings running wild, only letting them out in shy smiles,
your mind made up, it's competent,
you've waited for weeks to feel their breath against your cheeks.
Hands in hands, nose to nose, you can't write fast enough about
how strong these feelings grow.

Thoughts kept in your chest, sleepless nights,
mornings of unrest.
How will you explain the melting of your brain,
every time they pick up the phone, softly say your name,
London was calling and so was the rain, your heart kept itself
open, just in case.

I walked out West to try and understand why it takes a
heart so long to reset
you told me I was brave, even when I was in my weakest
state.

The way we let our emotions be managed, left a lot of
room for permanent damage,
there are pieces of us that we can salvage but I don't think
either of us could stand wading through the wreckage.
My heart was once held hostage by a person who thought
absence makes it grow fonder, all my mind did was wander.

The shackles fell away, my nights no longer a constant
melee, peace was found between my heart and mind,
I walked West to heal my heart best,
I did it in stillness,
in rest,
I healed it when I stopped looking for excess,
it was in saying goodbye to someone I thought I knew well,
emerging from my own little hell,
a person no longer held captive in their shell.

I walked past a place
the scent reminded me of a boy I used to crave,
of strong calloused hands around my waist,
in my mind acoustic guitars would play
as quickly as they'd come they'd fade away.
It was nice to live in the space,
at least for a moment,
for at least one more day.

THE MOMENT I KNEW

In a field underneath the powerlines
I knew everything would turn out fine -
things between you and I
the world would stop ending
we would all begin to try.
It came in slow moments
in universal signs,
from the lady bug on my thigh to the butterflies,
it was the dragonfly that kissed my cheek
it was the way the river turned softly in the creek.

RED LIGHT, GREEN LIGHT

They kiss in cars,
hold the face of their lover,
laughter without any care for what comes after,
the lights change,
faces stay the same.

Traffic stalls, time slows,
nobody else in the world needs to know,
the feelings are for you two alone,
kiss her while the lights are red, when they turn green,
kiss him like this is what the world has been waiting to see.

DATE YOUR FRIENDS

We lose track of time,
our days intertwine, this time together is a treasured moment of
mine.
Memories made together with no concern of the forecast, we
reminise the past, our struggles we will weather.
Skating down the street, ripped shoes, dirty knees, all our fun comes
for free. We have breakfast in the afternoon, cocktails under a waning
moon, your hand in mine and our journey intertwined.
Activities aplenty, I want to experience the world with you, crying
about our heartbreak and celebrating our swoons, I feel ever so lucky
to be appreciated by you.

It doesn't matter if we are far apart or if we a pressed nose to nose,
heart to heart, my devotion surrounds you every single day, even
though you may not come home to stay.

You would play Star Wars on the piano when I'd leave the
room to elicit a laugh out of me.
Through the wall I could hear you, humming, drumming,
softly softly, to yourself without the prescence of someone
else.

You would play Billy Joel with a pair of drunken birthday
eyes staring into my soul, your smile so wide, your excitement
something you couldn't hide.
You told me you'd hold me when we both got cold, wrap me
under the blanket fort you made so delicately, it was how you
whispered *I've got you, baby.*

WILL YOU GO TO THE PROM WITH ME?

Mountains nestle under clouds
I nestle under the weight of you,
a black dog cosies up to our door
while fantails search the underbrush for more,
their favourite bugs have been hidden since June.

Run towards the shoreline,
have a wine or a few,
bare your soul to the highlands,
walking for miles in step with you,
I would go anywhere across this planet if you asked me to.

Smiles hidden behind a coffee cup,
my eyes glued to a landscape
and a beautiful face
my comfort
my safest space.

MAMA

Heads rest in your lap, long fingernails run up and down a sleeping ball,
you always have the ability to take on our battles when we are too exhausted to fight back. We grew up, we grew tall, you still settle us down with no effort at all.
Our love runs deep, our love runs true, we wouldn't be anything without the strength and power of you.
There aren't enough words to describe the immense love you provide, the home you have built within us, how you take everything within your stride.
You are our life, you are our pride,
because of you, pure love has survived.

THE GROVE

Light in the early morning, birds are softly calling,
it's lemons in the trees, it's knocking bruised knees,
the morning sun baking our skin at twenty five degrees.
The breeze whispers softly to me, while you make us breakfast
abundantly,
'can you pick me a lime?'
you're one of a kind,
can I stay here and spend more time?

NEW LANDS

Neighbours call in Italian,
grandchildren are waiting,
hoping to be showered with love and delicate sweet bread.
Kisses upon foreheads, money discreetly tucked into pockets,
if mum and dad ask, you don't know where you got it.

Love spans generations, holding close the dearly departed,
if you wish to see it, look to the constallations
there you will find the weaving of the full hearted.
Kitchens vibrant, the aromas and colours of a homeland,
brought to new shores. The sounds of love wrapped around
the ears of those to come.

Mothers at the park speak in Vietnamese, they wave at the
women from the Middle East, their communities connected
by the new found ease a different place brings. Food is shared
upon a communal table, a bench laid out for those who are
hungry and available.

We are all connected - by love and by acts for another.
The land we reside on is not ours to claim, we are visitors upon
a place that will be here long after we've gone, but we are here
to protect and nuture it all the same.

KNOTS

Twists and turns,
my eyes blur, still,I cast my eyes upon a glowing sight,
my days feel light,
oh how I almost forgot,
a dizzying excitement, your whole world stops,
and that falling in love turns your stomach to knots.

SEVEN YEARS IN HEAVEN

We were so young when we met, my mind undedcided,
your heart was set. You were one of the most exciting
adventures of my life, a person so divine, I watched us both
grow and together, shine.
Not every road was easy, as we grew, we tried, I cried, we
fell apart. Our love, we attempted to keep it alive, put
everything on the line, but this time was goodbye.

But look at us now - you, ever beautiful you, how you have
eclipsed the expectations set before you. A love by your
side, a new adventure for your transforming life.
Don't lose faith - for you, I will always hold the space.

One of the greatest loves of my lifetime, I am so proud,
ever so lucky to have called you mine.

I will never know a first love like this again, one where you
are so warpped up in each other, your soul, your bestfriend.
Years may pass, lovers will dip in and out of beds, a piece of
you still resides in my hearts depths.
Seven years in heaven, a small price to pay, a true love is
deep and will never slip away.

NORTH STAR

Sweetheart you don't have to look far,
for the thing that sets you apart, for something that opens your
heart,
something simple or bizarre,
what you know to be your north star.
It shows you where to go, it will always guide you back home,
your path is predestined some may claim, do not fear,
do not distain, you will have choices all the same.
What you choose is up to you, you'll eventually figure out the
right thing to do.
Your heart will pine and your mind may waiver,
but your soul will always listen to its saviour.

Trust in what you know to be true,
good things are always seeking you,
there is magic in the mundane,
the world is wide but so is the space for you to claim,
be bold in your choices and make your mark upon the terrain.

Never forget that you are here, even though living can cause
you fear, know that I am with you, side by side we can hold
together, for I feel the same way too.

You are loved, you are cherished, you are not living just to
perish, you are smart and you are kind, you are here to speak
your mind.

Know you are special, know you are worthy, these words are
not here to hold you down, do not sink, do not drown.
You are alive and that's enough, be here today, worry less
about everyone else and their stuff.

LAUNDROMAT

Do you have a coin or two?

In the sky is a low hanging sun, holding out just for me and
you.
Floral soap, a broken dryer, old classifieds filled with hope.
Perched on an old wooden table, watching as dryers whirl,
unstable, your hands either side of my cheeks, kissing my face
until we hear the door creak.

We waited all afternoon for something to do, could we end
it with a bowl of soup, icream and one kiss - maybe even a
few? A mundane activity, perhaps, but I'd do it all over again
if you'd ask me to.

I can't take my eyes from your face, this feeling is one I
continue to chase. Your t-shirt white, your pants navy blue,
'Jesus Christ, I'm so into you.'

In solace we find the rest we need,
our mind turns to quiet,
no longer do we riot,
we are safe in the sound of stillness.

Breathe deeply,
listen carefully,
your true self is calling back home,
are you listening?

PLUNGE

You say nobody has really seen the truest you,
that you are reserved, quiet, not here for a romance riot,
I wade in the waters of this truth,
I plunge into the depths of you,
I am consumed.

You hide yourself away in a hope that you won't have your
heart break,
love is hard to come by, lust is easy to fake,
it takes you time to open up,
to soften down,
in me there is a trust you have found.

Quickly your heart found mine,
patiently coming back to life,
you did not fall gently,
you leapt off the deep end
a love willing to transcend
no more playing pretend.
I wade in the waters of this truth,
I plunge into the depths of you,
my heart open, yours now too.

You asked me about the colour of my eyes, if they were blue
or grey, what secrets did they keep, what feelings would arise;
how did they look when I was dreaming of my one true life.

You looked into my eyes, yours piercing and blue, I tried to
deflect, you sought after the truth. Your hands around a coffee
cup, your lips curved into a smirk, I knew you weren't going to
give this up.
You told me they lit up when I talked about things I wanted to
achieve, you didn't interrupt, you left room for me to breathe,
they changed from grey to green, out of excitement it must
be.

Yours are blue, the most intense I've seen, the colour of the
ocean, just the way that you want them to be.
Lost in conversation, your words slow and conscise,
eyes directly into mine, nowhere else to be,
me lost in you, out at sea.

You are the hill I choose to die on
I hope that is enough,
I would choose you in this lifetime and every single other one.

I sat by the river to write hoping inspiration would strike,
an older man sat beside me and pulled out a small easel
he was quiet, his hands weren't that nimble, he asked if it was a
problem to sit down, I replied there's more than enough space
to go around.
He began to paint a water colour scene,
one that would have fit on a Ghibli movie screen,
he told me he loved the autumn months, how the dust would
settle and leaves would crunch.
As soon as his tiny brush hit the paper, his hands did not
waver, he said that much like the colour of the trees, he was
waiting for his life to change.
Maybe he would find it in his scene
maybe I, upon this page.

You are not a secret to be kept
while someone figures out 'how to be their best.'
You deserve someone who will say your mess is my mess,
not a space where you feel your emotions are just a test.
You are not a secondary plan,
waiting day and night for someone to make up their mind
waiting until they're 'a decent man.'
You are a force majeure, someone we adore, like nobody else that
has come before.

WATERBABY

Merri creek isn't as bleak
as a lot of you make it out to be
wattle is blooming, ducks are crooning and babies grin wide.
The kissing of wind and the lush green of her leaves,
the sun on my skin and tranquil serenity,
have done more for me than hours of therapy.

I walk for hours upon the track,
a dog by my side,
we never look back,
behind us a city that doesn't sleep,
waiting for the next biggest brightest thing.

I walk in reverence,
expansive wilderness so generous,
somehow it feels secluded, intimate, abundant.
I breathe in the air, I soak up the light,
there is space here to forget, to dream, to call upon intention,
you are welcome here, upon the track, in the water and
amongst the greenery.
Hearts are cleansed, renewed and safe,
take in nature, own your space.

You call and ask about my day, about my life, you say *good
afternoon my love, my wife!'*
We are connected by love, faith, by a friendship that feels so
right, you know that you can talk to me at any time, day or
night.
I see you most days, a hug in passing, a kiss in the air, tell me
your problems, I can feel your pain from over there.
We are both trying to make it, to fumble our way through life,
there is no respite from the drama of our life, no repreave.
It's been three hours - just a phone, you and I,
I treasure this time, our minds we unwind,
I would sit here for hours with you, just to listen to you
breathe.

CARLTON

A street of revving cars and coffee machines,
hand held lovers in the lush green park,
one gentle afternoon,
a steaming bowl of soup,
it's the sight of you, you, you.
My breath caught in my chest,
you in a sunlit sillhouette,
taking you in, just for a moment,
mental snapshot, this I don't want to forget.

FAMILIA

I see our little house
our broken wooden fence,
me and you together
my reassurance, my safe space,
it just makes sense.

It is not blood that binds us together,
it's love, a trust, a look in your eyes,
your heartbeat in time with mine,
both of us knowing it's going to keep getting better.

You are my family,
you are my home,
the ones I am lucky enough to call my own,
no matter how far you go,
where your hearts wish to roam,
I'll be right here whenever you need me most.

Chaos

You made me weak in the knees
but I needed someone with stability,
someone to keep my head above the water
I didn't need rain in the middle of December,
I needed something more profound
I needed someone with their feet on solid ground.

Words spill unfound
from an unwise mouth,
dripping with meaning
gleaming teeth of wolves growling at my door,
anticipating that I'll give them more
while my spirit lies crushed on a dark wood floor.

Every word I write is a love letter to you
it breaks my heart in two,
for you cannot see how much I truly loved you.
You fight it in your head
wishing they were about another instead
yet they have always been for you
the good, the bad and my hands bleeding true.

Landscape of the heart,
pick me apart, show me the downfall of my relationship arc,
show me lovers I left behind in the dark.
Rocky terrain,
drumming hearts that will never be the same,
hold me through the night, shelter me from the pain,
that was caused by the slipping of another lovers name.

Christmas trees on a front lawn in January
lonely and forgotten,
rotting in a place where pines could never grow
discarded festive cheer thrown onto the side of the road.
How did we get to a place where things that were built to last,
end up beautifully wrapped, celebrated then left as trash.
Do we hold life in so little regard,
renounce things when they get hard, so that we can have a
bigger part in the madness of life?

What comes from your fingertips
boy I think you need a therapist,
the words you speak are unhinged.
To a false narrative, you cling,
hoping that you will be the one to win
a game that only you are playing.

You told me to have empathy -
I would fight the moon to change the tides
I could sink ships to the depth of the sea
with the amount of emotion that pours out of me.

We wax and we wane,
we fight and we feign interest in keeping this love alive,
the crescent is only present when I can feel myself slipping
away.

I loved you harder in September
when I felt like it wasn't going to get better,
I tried to keep us together, hands grasping at the waning threads
of us.
A birthday month, wrapped up in us, clothes like discarded gift
wrap on your bedroom floor, maybe we can make this work
once more.

Finches tapped at my window, bees knocked against my door, it
smelled like gardenias, mowed grass.
The sun glowed by lake, a springtime haze, there was something
in your narrow gaze.

I loved you with a ferocity that tore us apart, a parting gift,
a set of broken hearts.

GHOSTS OF CHRISTMAS PAST

Home alone on Christmas Eve
hanging what would have been our first wreath,
wrapped gifts placed under a big fir tree
no mistletoe kisses this year for me.
Red wine in a glass as a treat
ironic for someone who doesn't drink,
falling asleep in the summers heat
your skin was the only thing that was able to cool me.

Thoughts that held me down
now set me free,
I'll do Christmas with you around
and you will have a life without me,
then we'll see who felt more lonely.

EASY

You said it was hard for you to move on
from the love that used to be your number one
do you think it was easy for me?
Thinking I'm out flying free
I'm miserable as could be
it's taken me two years to figure out what happened to us
now even in the third
I haven't come up with much.

You told me you'd found someone new -
I was genuinely excited for you
then you changed your mind, wanted me by your side,
excuse me while I render myself confused.
It took me a while to understand
the mind of a man
who didn't take the time to understand
that I was grieving too, since I always end up coming back to
you.

It took me time to understand the heart of a man
who only thought of me as his secondary plan.

I feel the changing weather in my lungs,
I hear songs and sweet letters from those who I've long loved
and hexes of those I've wronged.

MUSEUM AND YOU

I skated back and forth outside the museum staring up at the
moon
trying to drown out the thoughts of you
an endless replay of conversations in my head
I knew it would never end.
A board with creaking wheels
couldn't help turn my emotions to steel
or change them into something I would no longer feel.
I turned endlessly in circles
weaving through barriers, mental and physical,
hoping that there would be meaning in the literal
waiting for my mind to settle
for my heart to ease, for longing to be exhaled in peace.

You say seeing me makes you sad
you think that in some way I must be glad
to be living my life without what we had.
You say I made you cry
yet I do not think that you comprehend
on that day we said our final goodbye
was the day my heart decided to die.

I do my best to find solace in quiet rest
yet every time I close my eyes
there you are, face firmly pressed
against the backs of my eyelids, with a smile only I can know
eating away at the love that will never grow.

I continue to give away loving parts of me
to those who cannot decide if they wish to stay or leave
trickles of salt down my face, tracing the lines of wearied age,
my own hands wrapped around a no longer 23-inch waist
wondering if I'd finally lost the one thing they wished to chase.

My body is merely a commodity
something they wish to put in their trophy case.

Imprinted half-moons in the creases of my palm
a distaste for what I see
a sign of my disgrace
why couldn't I be the one to hold myself in place under the
weight of another's gaze?

I suppose I am selfish when it comes to you
how could anyone ever know you the way I do?
The way your body moves, the way that you crack your neck,
how you would roll out of your side of the bed.
Jealousy for the one I used to be, lingers in my body
for she knew you better back then
than I ever will again.

There is a distrust
a disgust
of something, I hold dear: a heart, lungs, a brain, eyes and ears.
Something I should not shame to be,
how did I ever let the perceived value of another
determine the weight of me?

Making something that's not about you
Lord knows I've tried
but you are the one I've chosen to immortalise.

Slurpees we drank too quickly
blue and red they'd freeze our brain
I wish I could do the same with the pain,
press my tongue to the roof of my mouth.
rub my temples and sigh it out.

It would take less time
than watching the world pass me by
as my heart holds into something that isn't there.

I see you behind my eyes
your laugh, your crinkle lines
you are my full moon
my garden in full bloom
the dew in the morning
and the sun when it's dawning.
You're all I can think about
even months after you're gone,
I think because deep down
somewhere beneath the chasm in my chest
I knew you were probably the next one.

I turned my back on the sun
because it led me to you,
it showed me that you could have been the one
if you didn't still have growing up to do.

I turned towards the moon
for she was always good at obstructing the view
of boys with hearts that seemed true,
but you didn't mean as much to them
as they meant to you.

Your car is the closest to my house it's been in two years yet you've never felt farther away.

NOSTALGIA WILL KILL ME

I heard a couple by the river
they were speaking in hushed tones
they tried not to let others hear how they would argue
just like we used to.
It made me remember how I would cry
you would try to understand our mind,
I would forgive you,
you would hold my hands and kiss me slow,
it made me long for before,
when all I knew was the torture of you.

My knees buckled
the shower ran cold
I became reacquainted with my bathroom floor,
my shins are bruised blue
my lungs silently scream out for you
lips are cracked, water runs down my back
will I ever be washed anew?

My friends lovingly tell me to get over you, find someone new,
stop sulking over *this one.*
That's a lot easier said than done.
I know they mean well and want me to be happy
but love does not come off in the wash, it cannot be placed
kerbside and picked up the next morning,
removed as quickly as it was put down
it comes silent and without warning,
it leaves you in eternal mourning.

I bury your name with the love that you never gave.

For a new life, you must pay the price, a sweet little sacrifice.

My mind drifts to you
as I lay silently on the floor of a stranger's living room
my feet cold on hardwood floors, a rug scratching the back of my
neck
nose filled with lemon balm perfume
it is a ruthless thing to be so out of sorts when you were once so
sure.

Somewhere between comfort and chaos is where my heart and
mind both get lost, they fall into a pit which is non-descript, I
know that they are meant for more.
I have spent more time pulling myself up, nails dragging across
the floor.

Knuckles bloody in the fight, I know I will be able to win the
war.

Here, I have made my home, a vast space of which I can roam.
From the ashes I rise, more than a thousand times,
there is strength in my heart and in my mind,
the delicate balance which I seek to find.

Falling through the morning -
easy
quiet
I kick and push out the thoughts of you, the ones that
scream inside of my head, clinging on until the bitter
end.

You see war and peace
stories of people trying to flee
it makes it hard to comprehend
that one thinks the other is just here to expend,
that life is not a beautiful thing
just another form of currency
we raise our voices, wait with bated breath
just to see what they will do next
in the end we're lighting vigils
praying for those that they condemned.

My mother cries
because my brain cannot decide
if it wishes me to be sad or fine
if it should live or die.
Her hard work of keeping me alive
tied up in how well I am able to lie
to ensure she does not continue to cry.

THE GREAT PROTECTOR

When I mention his name
I watch your face change
your eyes softly narrow
as if you want to hold him in a lung-ending embrace.

LONESOME FOR YOU

I stay lonesome for you
keep myself heartbroken and blue
hoping that one day
my love will be enough and true.
I stay lonesome for you
hoping you'll change your mind
one day at a time
that I'll be the one of your kind.

You once told me you could hear lions from your
bedroom
how roars would carry across the suburbs
down backstreets, over garden beds, through the park,
funny how you could hear a lion half a mile away
and not the heart beating next to you.

It seems to be
that I always attract lovers no good for me
they smell of citrus and wood
their affections are ones I've misunderstood.

STONECOLD

Sweet as a peach
so why are you always rotten to me?

I sat and cried
as I watched a family not ready to say goodbye
I silently wept
for a family, I didn't know
as they kissed goodbye their well-loved pet.

A girl of ten looked at me through the glass
her face kept asking why
face and eyes were never dry.

I heard her voice break as she opened the door
her best friend lay there wagging her tail, upon a blanket on
the floor.
An intimate moment I should not have shared
hard to do when you feel their sadness and how much they
care.

A silent humming from a fridge door
as they reminisced about the life their friend had before.
Our friend death helps us find what we took in our stride
longing, memories and a love that will live and never die

You said I could call you any time
that you would pick up, day or night
I guess this was just another thing I was denied.
I think you said it so sweetly
I believed you sincerely, what would cause you to lie?
I called you once or twice
because I thought it would be nice
to hear the voice of the one who kept me warm on cold winter nights.
To hear how you've been, what shows have you seen, how that sweet
girlfriend of yours is going.

I asked if we were still friends,
you said *'of course, why would it end?'*
I took the chance to pretend, but we both know that it's never going
to be the same,
I grew up,
you didn't change,
I refused to continue having my heart break.

I think of you
absentmindedly my eyes began to cry
knowing the feelings you once had for me have passed you
by.
I hope they return
before they have had time to dry
was it worth saying goodbye
just for us to wait for things to be perfect before we try,
every tear-soaked day
another reminder that I wasn't able to hold onto you
and what we had cultivated all throughout the month of
May.

I hold out my hands for you
like the autumn does waiting for June
silent and calm
another raindrop on its arm
or was it a tear?
In the sunlight, it isn't so clear.
An olive branch, a fireside laugh,
fingers entwined, glasses of wine,
another moment passes by, where I am not yours and you
are not mine.

You're just a rookie, I'm playing hooky
to know if you've been bewitched
by love and to hear you say you love me too.
I am grieving a place I'm never leaving, with my arms
bound to you
you're waiting for me to be the woman that you need
but I will never be able to see things the way you want
me to.
You're foolish to think
that my love would be the thing to sink.

ZODIAC FOR TODAY:

I call and you do not answer
emotion spills out of me
your voicemail the receiver, the only way I can hear the
sounds of you,
lingering silence & long distance between us - all this will
ever be,
I guess that's what happens when you date a Cancer.

Love is like a housefire
you will either make it out alive or you'll burn inside -
as they've always said, better to be better off safe than
dead.

We're just friends
until it all gets too much and we end up kissing
for we knew what we were both missing,
only bodies will comprehend that
for you I will always backbend.

Green eyes, little white lies
how long did it take to convince yourself they were
true?
Did you stop to think how they would affect me
or are you too wrapped up in yet another someone
that will never be enough for you?

There's a hole in the sky, the moon high, she is in
shine

you say you can't sleep yet never tell me why.
The ghost that haunts your dream, I hope it doesn't
whisper in your ear about me and what could have
been.
I fell asleep to the songs that remind me of you, this
is the closest I'll get.
Your music plays in my head, words you once said
to me,
now said to your new lover on my side of the bed.

SNAKE EYES

It was the final kiss you blew
that is how I knew -
an unfamiliar girl stood by your side
eyes glaring into mine
a kiss goodbye
but for the last time.

Mothers cradle newborn babies in the street
their frail arms outstretched looking for peace
they stand upon rubble, lives in a heap.
On the corner of what was once a busy street
left in pieces and blown to bits
the sound is off and yet there are moving mouths
even with silence like this, you can tell it's bleak.

I've seen where your head used to lay and I've heard the
way she says your name,
the one who keeps your heart locked in a trap, how
could I ever compete with that?

The sky turns from black to grey
my lungs feel heavy, my throat blocked of all the things I
wish I could say
days grow colder, as does the shoulder pushing me away.

With eyes clouded green
a smile so pristine
I'm convinced I'm out of his league,
intrigue for what could potentially be
an ongoing wound, that will never rinse clean.
Does this happen to everyone or is it just me?

MY PERSON, YOUR TIME.

You told me you always hated the term right person wrong time,
it was always just another cheap line, made for people who couldn't make up their mind.
But you said it applied to us, we walked a very fine line,
I always knew you could never be mine, your heart wrapped up in someone elses twine and I was always waiting for the stars to align.

You were right, I was love blind, your messy mind and my inability to say goodbye.
Right person, wrong time,
a little death in our collective life.

I stood in the rain and cried
unintentional
but I've heard crying is really good for your soul.
I'm a water sign so maybe it'll be the thing that makes me
feel alive.
I drove home in silence, my car the only place I can stand
for it to be this quiet.

Watching the lights go from yellow to red the same way my
heart went from open to dead,
lungs rotting from the inside out
a thin cigarette in my hands and songs to cry to,
all my loved ones want is for me to forget about you
I didn't think it could be this hard to do.

You are wrapped within my skin, a light unable to dim, my knees
are bruised, stuck between a love you're unable to lose.
I didn't think my eyes would run this much over missing the
warmth of your touch, the way you talk in your sleep or how
much you'd end up meaning to me.

What a mess I've created for myself, another book stacked on
your shelf, a melody you have discarded, one you thought you
couldn't part with.

HODDLE STREET OR SOMEWHERE INBETWEEN

I wish you would have told me that you were in someone
else's sheets
so I wouldn't be left here waiting in a purgatory of you and
me, what could have been, a long-gone distant fantasy.
It would have been nice to know, instead of simply
guessing.
The look she gave, was the one your ex once gave me,
once again knowing how it feels to be the one in the
middle of you and your new baby.
I suppose I'll always be the one in between, a stepping
stone to the one you need, hopeless and romantic
chewing my lips until they bleed.

Though you are blind you can still see
the affections and longing of another & feelings that are
still coming from me.
Your knees touched, a quick brush, perhaps I wouldn't see
you drove them home, my heart sank and that was
enough for me.

YOU'RE ALL INVITED

I'm not sure if this will make it better or worse
just throw my body bag into a hearse.
Drive me around the suburbs I used to love
before my heart went and fucked everything up.
Show me what I'm going to miss - coffee when we hear
the rain, haircuts in the kitchen, a Christmas tree we
would decorate, the fairy lights and songs that make us
kiss.

The funeral is tomorrow, bring everyone you know, show
them what happens when you let your unrequited love
grow, it'll be a party, a celebration, make sure that you've
got your invitation.

Standing room only, make sure you wave the car
goodbye, you only get a few chances at this, don't let
them pass you by.

Has it been raining?
No,
my shirt is soaked through
drip drop, forget me not
lost myself again thinking of you.

We ended it because you had things to figure out
we ended it because I had inner work to do
you didn't want to fuck us up
yet you've fallen into the arms of someone new, funny how
you went seeking all the things I was willing to give you.

We ended it because the timing wasn't right, I cried for
months each night, was I not enough or too much? Is it
because I cut my hair? Because I told you how much I care?
Or was it because I wasn't in the next suburb?

If you weren't ready you should have said, instead of leading
me to think that eventually, we'd be sleeping together in the
same bed, for more than one weekend.

ALWAYS SECONDARY

She is similar to me, in looks and personality, though she's only 5'3.
Her hair also unruly, eyes not glassy, she is who I was before my tears began to pool, before I fell in love with you.

Was I too heavy to hold? Just someone with a burdensome soul?
I bet she's lighter in your arms when you cradle her at night, the same way you held me only a few months ago.

Do you only want me when the when there is nothing left to catch your eye, when all of the seemingly pretty things have passed you by? Do you only want me when there's nothing else, when I'm the one to fill the emptiness of your lonely nights?

These lands were green as far as the eye can see
they made me think of him and how his eyes would always gleam,
especially when he looked at me.

Merry Christmas you said
two days later you left,
I drank gin in somebody else's home
alone,
happy New Year's to me.

It would be easy for you to say that you love me
but to say it with such certainty,
that is something that would weigh heavy
even upon your strong shoulders.
The words don't get any easier
even though we get older.

Now that would is be a sight to see,
you saying something that you truly mean.

I ran eyes shut towards New South Wales
its arms like beaches, open wide
Her weather wet and my eyes not kept dry.
For days it rained and I began to change
my outer self starting to fade, the inside anew.

The closer I got to the border the harder it became to come
home,
my mind remembering the reasons I left,
what you had said,
my insides churning and my heart fighting to stay away,
maybe I could live here another day.
Start a new life,
somebody bring my dog,
let my mind dispel the fog,
the shore taking with it the memories that came before.

UNRAVEL

I feel myself unravelling little by little as if someone is pulling out
a thread with tiny pins and needles
my heart no longer nimble.
I unravelled myself from my bones
from all the versions of me that I'd ever known,
falling away from what felt like home.

You used to offer to drive me home
now I'm sitting in my car all alone,
it might be romantic if there was snow
but it's just another hail storm hitting my window.
Your voice called out to me in a dream, soft, sweet, humbling
just like I remember it to be.

AROMA OF YOU

I can't bear the scent of Santal 33
it makes me think of summertime,
every girl I've ever known
and the everlasting image of you,
who you have become,
& the day you finally said goodbye to me.

I would have married you
not because you asked me to
but because I couldn't see myself living through these days
without you.
I'd rather be alone
than give love to someone who hasn't yet grown.

It seems I am always waiting for someone to show
the same love and care for me, that I give away so freely
they are always undeserving and it costs me dearly.

I know you would have married me
if my soul wasn't destined to run and leave,
because you said my eyes were the closest thing to emerald
green after watching that film and crying.

Maybe you were the one that got away
maybe I was the one who wasn't destined to stay.

A continual screeching in my ears
of all the love lost and wasted throughout the years,
when did I let it affect my happiness?
I'm tongue-tied, I'm tough
I'm trying my best not to speak so rough,
I'm sad and I'm soft
I'm trying not to think too much,
I'm diving in, I'm on the cusp
of something that makes me feel better than good enough.

To the one that comes next, don't play with my heart so rough
tell me you won't, oh tell me you won't.

I left myself behind
I thought I would have changed with time,
walking through fire and coming out the other side
I thought I would be fine.
I put my soul on the line and trusted you every time
my heart gave out before my spine,
I waited for you, for my eyes to dry.
Packing up all I knew and leaving it discarded to the night
I left myself behind,
I thought I could have spared myself this time.

Your piano taps into the ghosts that used to roam the halls
before I arrived,
they send out little morse codes
hoping that they'll reach those that meant more.
A rhythmic love that I am not above
tiny keys hoping to shake the teeth of the souls that you buried
underneath,
hearts that belong to another home
while your little keys sing out to them all alone.

My girlfriend, my girlfriend, my girlfriend he mumbled in his
sleep
My girl, my girl, he sang it to the world
My friend is what I became in the end.

TRAITOR

The image of the two of you on the beach
runs through my mind, while I drove home, my best friend was
on the line, weeping eyes unable to dry.
I didn't sleep for weeks
it seemed not to matter to you,
you seemed to forget us as quickly
as the waves came in and out of the shore,
maybe I fell too hard
maybe I was a bore
but I think it's because you were still longing for what you had
before.

If I let you dance on my grave
would that make us okay?
Would you want to run or would it make you want to stay?

LOVE MOTEL

Your heart has no vacancy
no time for me
is it because I've shown you the possibility of what a safe home
and tethered love could be?

On the ninth I was by your side by the eleventh we said goodbye,
I didn't think we would be this cut and dry, hang my love outside
and we can both watch as you bleed me dry.
I don't know what it's gonna take for me to learn my lesson this
time.

4 A.M CONFESSIONS

I've fallen in love with you
irresponsibly so
in a way, I am still coming to know
there is nothing more to it than that
this love is a statement, a fact
take it how you want it
or give it back to me in a paper bag,
whatever I need will come to be,
they say the universe always has your back.

Where was the universe when I was grieving something I once knew?

We sat by the creek, your hand dipping in an out of the water
you hadn't slept for a week
I gaze upon your sunburnt shoulder, when was the last time you
felt real laughter?
Days grow into night and your demeanour becomes colder
I keep silent, I'm too tired to put up a fight,
your hands wet, the stage is set for a love that even we could not
foster.

You were excited when you heard that I was going to move house, now a few suburbs closer to you, is this because we're friends once again or because it makes it easier for a midnight rendezvous?

You told me that your friends described you as a young and single guy, I kept my eyes fixed upon a monstera, you looked at me apologetic I think your brain regretted when your mouth said it.
All I could do was say *yeah I guess,* so helpless.

I constantly hear from people, how good-looking you are, I smile and say *truly beautiful,* another little knife straight through my heart.

I always nod and smile as they gush, for what else can I do, while I watch the rest of the world fall in love with you.

Dreaming, scheming, wasting my days believing.

We were over before we began
it's so typical
to fall in love with something non reciprocal
it's amazing that I haven't become cynical.

DEAREST VIOLETTA

Violetta,
did you get my letter?
Confessing how much I love the time we spent together,
I couldn't bring myself to bore you with details of the stormy
weather
only of how my heart is lifted and can feel my soul getting
better.

Oh Violetta,
how I miss when your eyes crinkle and the shape of your
dimple,
who knew falling for you would be this simple?

We met in late July under a rain cloud sky
I miss the shape of your waist, the caricature of your face,
I keep your picture in my wallet, close to my chest, safely
tucked into my breast pocket.

Oh Violetta,
I must confess, I haven't been my best, being this far from you
has caused me unrest.
If you could be so kind, to vacate yourself from my mind
I think that in time I will be able to pass on by
without eternal sorrow or a tear in my eye.

There's no timeline for grief
it lives in my throat, my chest and my sheets,
it grips you and drags you underneath.
Grief blurs your vision,
a new day, another tiny incision
making it to the surface is your mission.

Younger than me with nicer teeth
with skin so clear I could hardly breathe.
She's hardly different to me but I bet she smells so sweet,
unlike citrus and caffeine.

Trying to keep you is a race in which I can't compete,
I'll always be the thing you don't want
but the thing you come to need.
I've made my peace
with loving someone
who won't ever be ready for someone like me,
someone with love to give and rosy cheeks
with a heart of gold and kind words to speak.

I hope she makes you happy,
I'm not saying this superficially,
you deserve someone who loves who you've grown to be,
it's a shame it wasn't me,
but that's on you
and the relationship you gave away.

I hope you took her to the lake
and kissed her in the same place
where you said you hoped nothing between us would change.

We could be together in this space
blissfully unaware
knowing you were my safe place
sunlight even on the darkest of days.

Now you've gone
left what we had discarded far away
pushing aside a little love,
for the benefit of a sweeter face.

MAMA KNOWS

Your mother told you she liked me the best, of all the girls
you dated
I wasn't the one she hated,
she isn't easily pleased, you told me,
it was something the others hadn't achieved.
I think it's because I made you laugh
I tried my best from the start.
Because I kept you on some sort of track -
maybe it was in the way we would hold hands
or the way we included her in coffee plans.
I don't know why you told me this,
a few months after we said goodbye,
you told me that you agreed with her,
when she said I was one of the best things to happen to you,
I told you that I agree with her too.

Mama knows best,
but, I guess,
Mama also raised a fool.

www.ingramcontent.com/pod-product-compliance
Lightning Source LLC
Chambersburg PA
CBHW061113100726
47911CB00013B/521